The Emperor and the Nightingale

Retold by Rosie Dickins

Illustrated by
Graham Philpot

Reading Consultant: Alison Kelly
Roehampton University

The Emperor of China was
a very proud man. He
always wanted the
best of everything.

3

His palace was made of
fine white bricks. The roof
was solid gold.

The garden was full of
bright flowers with silver
bells. They tinkled in
the wind.

The garden was very big.
It was so big that even the
Emperor never saw it all.

Woof!

He never saw the little
brown nightingale who
lived in the trees.

7

But other people
saw the nightingale.

The gardener
saw her every
day. He liked to
listen to her singing.

Her songs always
made him smile.

One day, the Emperor was reading a book about his wonderful palace.

The book said: "*The garden is full of bells that tinkle sweetly.*"

The Emperor smiled –
but the next page made
him frown. It went on: *"But
the nightingale's song sounds
sweeter than the bells!"*

What's a
nightingale?

"Why haven't I heard this nightingale?" snapped the Emperor. "Bring it to sing in the palace – now!"

The palace servants never went into the garden. They didn't know anything about the nightingale. But they didn't dare tell the Emperor.

What's a nightingale?

Where can we find it?

They searched high and low. They looked under flowers...

and behind bushes.

Spiders can't sing!

In the end, they had to ask the gardener.

"I can show you the nightingale," he said.

Follow me...

They walked and walked.
Suddenly, they heard
a croak.

"The nightingale!"
cried the servants.

ribbit-ribbit

The gardener smiled. "No, that's a frog in the pond," he replied.

A little later, they heard
a loud **MOO**.

"The nightingale!"
shouted the servants.

"No, that's a cow in the field," the gardener told them. He was trying not to laugh.

19

In the end, they came
to a tree. Just then, the
nightingale began to sing.

Che-che-cheer ♪
♪ up! Cheer up! ♪

When she finished, the
servants clapped. "Little bird,
the Emperor wants you to
sing in his palace," they said.

21

"My songs sound best out here, among the trees," said the bird, "but I will come."

And she flew back to
the palace with them.

23

The Emperor was surprised to see such a little brown bird.

She's not very pretty!

But when she sang, he was enchanted by her voice.

24

The Emperor liked her
voice so much, he ordered
her to stay and sing to him
every day.

25

The Emperor gave the
nightingale a silver cage.
But she missed living
outside, among the trees.

Soon, the little brown bird was famous. Even the Emperor of Japan came to hear her sing.

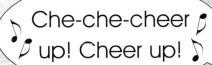

Che-che-cheer up! Cheer up!

What a sweet voice!

One day, a big box
arrived at the palace.

To: The Emperor
of China

Here's an even
better nightingale!

From: The Emperor
of Japan

Inside, there was another nightingale. This one had sparkling golden feathers. Its eyes were made of rubies.

When you turned a key,
it sang like the little brown
bird – well, sort of...

although the
tune was always
exactly the same.

The Emperor was very happy.

He was so happy, he forgot all about the little brown bird. She flew away – and nobody noticed.

Until one day,
instead of singing...

it went *whizz-whirr*
and *ker-plunk*.

33

Something had broken
inside. No one knew how
to fix it.

34

Now the Emperor longed
for the little brown bird.
But no one could find her –
not even the gardener.

Then the Emperor became
sick. He lay in bed, staring
sadly at his broken bird.

His room was full of
silence and shadows.
The doctors said he
was close to death.

Suddenly, the sound of birdsong filled the air. It was the real nightingale.

She had found out the
Emperor was sick. So she had
come back to sing for him.

She sang so sweetly that
the shadows seemed to fade.
The Emperor smiled – and
he began to get better.

Che-che-cheer
up! Cheer up!

Soon, the Emperor was
well again. "I'm sure the
nightingale cured me,"
he thought.

"Please stay," he begged the little bird. "You can have a golden cage and all the servants you want!"

I'll throw away the golden bird.

"I prefer to live outside among the trees," the nightingale replied. And she flew away.

The Emperor was very sad.
He asked the gardener to
plant a tree under his window.
"It will remind me of the
nightingale," he said.

The gardener watered
the tree every day. It grew
and grew.

One day, the Emperor
heard something flutter past
his window. He looked out.

To his surprise, he saw *two*
nightingales. They were
building a nest in the tree.

And when they sang,
everyone in the palace
smiled to hear them – the
Emperor most of all.

The story of the Emperor and the nightingale was first told by Hans Christian Andersen. He was born in Denmark in 1805, the son of a poor shoemaker. He left home at fourteen to seek his fortune and became famous all over the world as a writer of fairy tales.

Series editor: Lesley Sims

Designed by Louise Flutter

First published in 2007 by Usborne Publishing Ltd., Usborne House, 83-85 Saffron Hill, London EC1N 8RT, England. www.usborne.com
Copyright © 2007 Usborne Publishing Ltd.